STICKLEY STICKS TO IT!

for my parents and their gift of stick-to-it-ness—*BSM*

for Alex and Ava. Have the dedication and courage
to always stick to your dreams—*SM*

Published by
MAGINATION PRESS
An Educational Publishing Foundation Book
American Psychological Association
750 First Street, NE
Washington, DC 20002

For more information about our books, including a complete catalog, please write to us, call 1-800-374-2721, or visit our website at www.apa.org/pubs/magination.

Printed by Worzalla, Stevens Point, WI

Book design by Sandra Kimbell

Library of Congress Cataloging-in-Publication Data
Miles, Brenda.
Stickley sticks to it! : a frog's guide to getting things done / by Brenda S. Miles, PhD ;
illustrated by Steve Mack.
pages cm
"American Psychological Association."
Summary: When it comes to homework, projects, and goals,
Stickley the frog is a flexible thinker who never gives up.
Includes bibliographical references.
ISBN 978-1-4338-1910-0 (hardcover : alk. paper) — ISBN 1-4338-1910-4 (hardcover : alk. paper) —
ISBN 978-1-4338-1911-7 (pbk. : alk. paper) — ISBN 1-4338-1911-2 (pbk. : alk. paper)
[1. Perseverance (Ethics)—Fiction. 2. Frogs—Fiction.] I. Mack, Steve (Steve Page), illustrator. II. Title.
PZ7.M5942St 2014
[E]—dc23
2014034579

Manufactured in the United States of America
First printing October 2014
10 9 8 7 6 5 4 3 2 1

FSC
www.fsc.org
MIX
Paper from
responsible sources
FSC® C002589

STiCKLEY STiCKS TO iT!

A Frog's Guide to
Getting Things Done

by Brenda S. Miles, PhD

illustrated by Steve Mack

Magination Press • Washington, DC
American Psychological Association

Meet **STiCKLEY.** He's a frog.
Every day he wears shorts
and a fancy bowtie.

Stickley's toes are **STICKY,** and they work like suction cups. But Stickley is a frog, so sticky toes make sense.

Stickley has a gift.
It's called **STICK-TO-IT-NESS.**

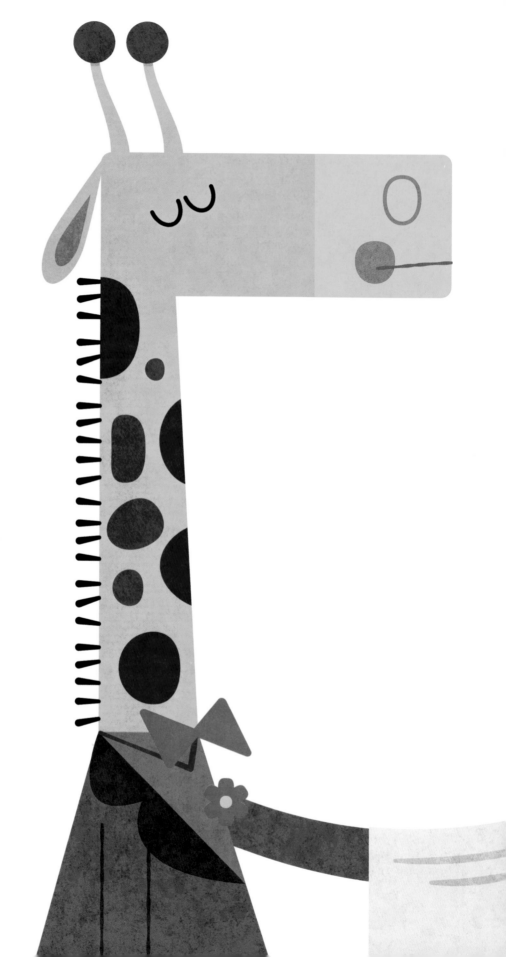

He can stick to windows and ceilings—even under **PLATES!**

But he upset guests in a fancy restaurant once, so he **NEVER** did that again!

Sometimes stick-to-it-ness **ANNOYS** Stickley—like when he kicks a soccer ball and it stays stuck on his toes.

Surfing can be tricky, too, when the waves
are **GIGANTIC** and he can't ditch his surfboard.

Stickley's **TOES** aren't the only way he sticks to things.

Stickley's **ATTITUDE** helps him stick to things, too, like projects and goals.

And that makes stick-to-it-ness mostly **GREAT** because it helps Stickley get things done.

Stickley tries his best and never gives up—even when work is hard—and that's a **BIG** part of stick-to-it-ness.

Did you know that Stickley won a trophy for spelling **ORANGUTAN** forwards and backwards? He took his time and stuck to it!

Octavia couldn't do it—and she's an orangutan! Clearly she didn't have Stickley's **STICK-TO-IT-NESS** on that day!

Stickley knows there are many ways to stick to almost anything. When he decides to do something—like build a tower—he makes a **PLAN** and **GATHERS SUPPLIES.**

When he feels tired, he takes a **BREAK.**

But sticking to it means going back to work **AFTER** his break, and Stickley **ALWAYS** does that.

When Stickley gets confused, he stops and thinks about the problem in a different way. He **LOOKS** at the problem in a different way, too!

Sometimes projects don't work out, but he makes a **NEW** plan and starts over.

If he's really stuck—in a **"CAN'T FIGURE IT OUT"** kind of way—he asks for help. Asking for help helps Stickley keep going. And when he keeps going...

...the results are

MAGNIFICENT!

When Stickley wrote a speech for school, he didn't give up either.

"I CAN DO THIS!" he said, because stick-to-it-ness means taking chances and believing in yourself—even when you're not sure what will happen.

First, he made a **PLaN.** "I'll talk about surfing!" He gathered materials.

When he felt tired, he took **BReaKS,** but he kept working after his breaks until he was finished.

But then, a problem—his speech was too long! The teacher wanted a 2-minute speech, not a 10-minute one! Stickley stopped to think about his speech in a **DiFFeReNT** way.

He made a **NEW** plan. He started over.

He asked his parents for ideas, too. "Maybe talk about why you **LOVE** surfing," they said, "and being tossed by **BIG** waves—up, down, and all around."

Suddenly, Stickley knew what to do. "I'll talk about surfing, but I'll **SHOW** my class, too!"

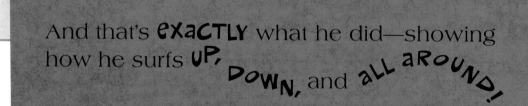

And that's **EXACTLY** what he did—showing how he surfs UP, DOWN, and aLL aROUND!

The class cheered! Stickley's speech had words **AND** actions—and it was **MAGNIFICENT!**

Now Stickley teaches the **WHOLE** class—even **OCTAVIA**—how to make a plan and stick to it!

STICK

NoTe To PaReNTS, CaReGiVeRS, aND TeaCHeRS

Stickley has the gift of *stick-to-it-ness.* Stick-to-it-ness is perseverance: the ability to stick with tasks and see them through, no matter how frustrating or challenging they may be, even when good results are not guaranteed. Parents, caregivers, and professionals who work with children are becoming more interested in skills like perseverance because getting things done at home and at school helps children achieve goals and feel proud.

SeLF-ReGuLaTioN

Perseverance is one aspect of *self-regulation.* Self-regulation includes many different skills like adjusting one's energy to fit a situation (e.g., being excited in gym class but calm during story time), staying focused and shifting attention when needed, planning and working through steps to get tasks done, managing emotions in ways that help us cope, and understanding social cues and situations so we respond effectively. Children who are skilled self-regulators can adjust well to expected and unexpected events that happen every day. They are also skilled at getting things done—taking initiative, devising plans and goals, rethinking strategies as problems arise, and monitoring progress—whether on school work, in social interactions, or on the sports field. When good self-regulators face challenges, they might feel angry or frustrated, but they don't let big emotions take charge. Instead, they are able to calm down, bounce back from disappointment, and persevere on challenging tasks with determination and confidence, just like Stickley!

Research shows that effective self-regulation is important for maintaining mental health, developing social skills, and achieving academic success. It also contributes to job success when children become teenagers and adults. That's why skills like persisting on tough tasks, being organized, regulating emotions, and cooperating with classmates often appear on report cards in addition to subjects like math and reading. These skills are just as important as academic achievement for success and mental health later on.

BRaiN DeVeLoPMeNT

Stick-to-it-ness and other self-regulation skills develop over time with learning and experience, and with the growth of the brain's *frontal lobes,* located behind the forehead. The frontal lobes help with tasks like focusing attention, stepping back and trying to make sense of situations so emotions don't take over, breaking big tasks into smaller ones, and predicting what might happen in the future. Stick-to-it-ness is also an important part of what frontal lobes do.

Children are not born with large doses of stick-to-it-ness—and that's perfectly normal. Skills like setting goals and sticking to them can improve with age, but children will still struggle with some tasks as they grow older because the frontal lobes are not yet mature. In fact, the frontal lobes are *still developing* when children are growing into teenagers and young adults! As the brain develops, tasks children can do easily and those they may struggle with will change over time. For example, a five-year-old might know that crayons and paper are required for a craft, but struggle with all the steps needed to get ready in the morning. A ten-year-old might get ready for school easily but struggle to start and finish a science fair project due in three weeks.

The good news is that you can help support—and fine-tune—your child's developing brain. A growing brain is shaped by many influences. Since the frontal lobes develop over a long stretch of time, you can help nurture stick-to-it-ness, and other self-regulation skills, that will last a lifetime.

STRaTeGieS FoR BooSTiNG STiCK-To-iT-NeSS

The most important way to nurture stick-to-it-ness is with kind and sensitive parenting. Praising your child's *efforts* rather than focusing on *outcomes* like winning or losing should help your child see value in trying his or her best—and sticking to it—no matter what. But sticking to it *does* mean getting things done and, along with your support, children often need concrete strategies to accomplish what they set out to do. The strategies Stickley uses might help you and your child boost stick-to-it-ness and get things done, too!

Make a plan and gather supplies. Help your child with big or small projects by devising a plan together and deciding

what supplies your child will need. Explain that big work gets easier when it is broken down into smaller chunks. Work of any size can be carved into smaller units. For example, a cluttered math sheet might be chunked by covering every row of problems except one—and only uncovering the second row when the first row has been completed.

For larger assignments, a big X on the calendar marking the due date probably won't promote stick-to-it-ness. Instead, sit down with your child, brainstorm all the parts of the assignment that need to be completed, and then divide the project into smaller *subgoals*. Anticipate challenges and gently guide your child with suggestions so the timelines and workloads are manageable. Next, create a visual schedule together, showing chunks of work that must be completed by specific dates. Children who are tech-savvy might prefer to create a schedule on a cell phone or computer with reminder alarms added. Encourage your child to check subgoals off the list as they are completed.

Gathering all the supplies needed for a project ahead of time—and putting them all in one place—might also help to minimize obstacles and make completing work easier.

Take a break. Attention is a limited resource, meaning adults and children have only so much of it before they need to recharge. Usually older children can focus longer than younger children, and adults can focus longer than teenagers, but people of all ages need breaks to re-energize the body and mind when sticking to anything. Build in *predictable breaks* so your child knows when they will

happen, and when they are over. It may be helpful to set a timer so your child knows when to expect breaks and how long those breaks will last. Children with attention difficulties will likely need *more breaks, more explicit instructions for working through tasks,* and *more subgoals* than children who can focus relatively easily on larger tasks at one time. *Regular, good quality sleep* is also important for boosting attention and stick-to-it-ness. Consult a medical doctor if you are concerned about your child's sleep, or unsure about how many hours of sleep your child needs each night.

Go back to work after a break. If you use a timer—or a natural break like dinnertime—it will be clear when your child should return to work. Though breaks help stick-to-it-ness last longer, *be careful not to overdo it.* After a full day of school, for example, working on a project could be exhausting. One break might be enough between two short work sessions, with the second break being bedtime! Try your best to monitor your child's energy levels so you know how many work sessions seem

reasonable. Breaking up projects over several days or weeks in the initial planning stage should also help to limit fatigue.

Stop and think about the problem in a different way. When obstacles happen—and they will—encourage your child to stop, step back, and think about the problem in a different way. Your child will probably need help at this stage. Provide suggestions, or direct modeling, depending on how much help your child needs. For example, if your child is struggling to write a speech, offering *specific ideas* to discuss—or *modeling how to write or say the ideas* so the audience stays interested—may be necessary.

Make a new plan. If you and your child make a new plan—particularly for a school assignment—map it out on a visual schedule, so new subgoals and deadlines are clear. Explain that changing the game plan is okay when a job is not working out as expected.

Ask for help. Help can boost stick-to-it-ness, but sometimes you might wonder if sitting down with your child and chunking tasks into smaller steps is providing *too much* help. After all, isn't your child old enough to know how to do these tasks and take responsibility for them?

Children won't automatically know all the steps—and the order in which to do them—for completing a chore or a school project. Some children can tackle big tasks fairly well, but many find planning, chunking, and sticking to it challenging. If you teach your children early on how to break

down tasks and stick to subgoals, then chances are your child's brain will begin to generate patterns for success on its own. When tasks are assigned, you want your child to think instinctively, "I'll need to make this task smaller and finish it over many days," whether your child is in elementary school or university. Learning steps from you should help boost this kind of thinking, so encourage your child to ask for help when it is needed.

When you do make suggestions, and your child still struggles, you may need to provide *even more assistance,* especially if fatigue is not the issue. Help can come in many forms. For example, if you explain all the steps needed to take out the trash—and you post those steps on a laminated schedule that your child can check off with an erasable marker as the steps are completed—then your child is still getting help but can work more independently, without consulting you at every step.

DO TOUGH STUFF TOGETHER

When your child struggles to persevere—or outright refuses to do something—you might wonder if that lack of stick-to-it-ness is *rather-not-do-it-ness* more than anything else. When tasks are big and challenging, most of us would rather not do them, whether we are 8 or 48! But many times a lack of motivation comes from being unsure about where to begin and how to keep going. Your child may never like doing homework or chores, but you might reduce some resistance by devising a clear process outlining what steps need to be done and how and when to do them. For cleaning a bedroom, for example, you could post steps, such as "1) put toys in bin, 2) put dirty clothes in hamper, 3) make the bed." Breaking a task down into steps should make the process more straightforward and easier to follow. Setting a *specific routine* for chore and homework time may also help your child know what to expect and prepare to stick to it each day when necessary. Remember, too, that children model what they see. When you tackle your own tough work, like cleaning or completing office work at home, persevere with a positive attitude. Consider doing tough stuff together so everyone at home is working at the same time. Chant "Stickley sticks to it! That's how he gets through it!" every now and again to boost morale!

ADDITIONAL SUPPORT

For more information on supporting your child's stick-to-it-ness at school, read *School Made Easier: A Kid's Guide to Study Strategies and Anxiety-Busting Tools* (2014) by Wendy L. Moss, PhD, and Robin A. DeLuca-Acconi, LCSW, published by Magination Press. Written for students 8 to 13 years old, the book offers tips for getting organized, breaking down assignments into smaller steps, managing time effectively, and other ideas for succeeding at school.

In all likelihood, you are the best resource for helping your child develop stick-to-it-ness. However, if your child continues to struggle with organization and planning, focusing on tasks, or managing emotions, it may be helpful to consult a licensed psychologist or other mental health professional.

ABOUT THE AUTHOR

Brenda S. Miles, PhD, is a pediatric neuropsychologist who has worked in hospital, rehabilitation, and school settings. She believes that the words "work harder" don't really work. Instead, she recommends "Let's step back for a moment and think about how we can get this work done!" She is the author of two other books for children, *Imagine a Rainbow: A Child's Guide for Soothing Pain,* and *How I Learn: A Kid's Guide to Learning Disability,* both published by Magination Press.

ABOUT THE ILLUSTRATOR

Steve Mack grew up a prairie boy on Canada's Great Plains and has drawn for as long as he can remember. His first lessons in art were taught to him by watching his grandfather do paint-by-numbers at the summer cottage. He has worked for greeting card companies and has illustrated several books. Steve lives in a beautiful valley in a turn-of-the-century farmhouse with his wife and two children. Steve and his children love catching frogs by the river close to their house. They haven't found any frogs with Bermuda shorts on yet...

ABOUT MAGINATION PRESS

Magination Press is an imprint of the American Psychological Association, the largest scientific and professional organization representing psychologists in the United States and the largest association of psychologists worldwide.

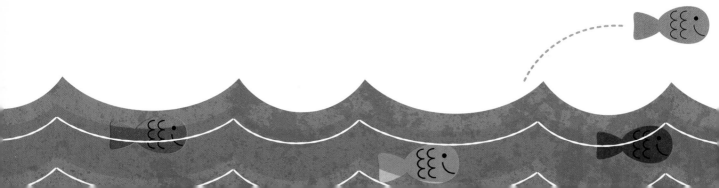